Where is Maria?

Where is Maria?

By Louise Gunther

Drawings by Helen Cogancherry

GARRARD PUBLISHING COMPANY
CHAMPAIGN, ILLINOIS

To Deborah Yaffe,
photographer and friend,
for all the street fairs
we've enjoyed together

Library of Congress Cataloging in Publication Data

Gunther, Louise.
  Where is Maria?

  (For real)
  SUMMARY: Three persons looking for Maria enjoy the
fun of a street fair and finally spot the lost girl
from the top of a ride.
  [1. Fairs—Fiction] I. Cogancherry, Helen.
II. Title.

PZ7.G9812Wh   [E]   79-11733
ISBN 0-8116-4311-5

Where is Maria?

Rose and Anna came out the door.
Mike was putting up a sign
for the fair.
"How do you like it?"
he asked the girls.

"Neat," said Rose.
They helped him put signs
up and down the streets.
"I can't wait until Saturday,"
Rose told Anna.

Saturday morning
Rose and Anna got up early.
"Look," said Anna.
"Some tables are set up already."

Mrs. Sanchez waved to them.

"Can we help you, Mrs. Sanchez?"
called the girls.

"Yes," said Mrs. Sanchez.

"Would you bring me the plants
that are inside the door."

"Everyone will want to buy
your pretty plants," said Anna.

"Thank you, girls,"
said Mrs. Sanchez.

"Did you know
my niece is coming?
You'll like Maria."

"Great," said Rose.

"We'll come back later," said Anna.

More and more people
were setting up tables.

DRAWINGS of the
FAIR by ROSE
and ANNA
10¢ each

Rose and Anna
set up their table too.
Then Rose helped her mother.

Anna helped her parents
set up their table.
"I made a sign for you,"
she said.
"What a great sign,"
said her father.
He put it
where everyone could see it.

"Look," Rose shouted to Anna.
"Dad is riding in the Flying Turtle."
She pointed down the street.
"When can we have a ride?"
the girls called.
"As soon as I get off," he said.

He gave them each a ticket.
They climbed into the Flying Turtle.
"This is my favorite ride,"
shouted Rose.
"Wheeeeee!" cried Anna.
"What can we do next?"

A lot of people
had come to the fair.
"It's time for us
to draw some pictures,"
Rose told Anna.
The girls put on their signs.

BOOKS

G HING CHINESE RESTAURANT

EGG ROLL
10¢

BASKETS

They took their pads and crayons.
"Drawing pictures will be fun,"
said Anna.
"And we can walk everywhere
and see everything," said Rose.
First Anna drew a picture
of Mrs. Sanchez's plants.

"This is a lovely picture,"
said Mrs. Sanchez.
"How much is it?"
"It's ten cents,"
said Anna and Rose.
Mrs. Sanchez paid them.
"Where is Maria?" asked Anna.
"I don't know," said Mrs. Sanchez.
"I'm worried about her.
She should be here by now."
"Maybe the bus broke down,"
said Rose.
"We'll come back later."
The girls drew more pictures.
"There's Oscar," shouted Anna.
"Let's go buy an egg roll."
"It's ten cents," said Oscar.

"I'll buy that picture,"
said Mr. Wong.
"They're ten cents too,"
said Anna.
Oscar gave the dime
back to Anna.
"This is nicer than a photo,"
said Mrs. Wong.

"We'll see you later, Oscar,"
said the girls.
Rose and Anna sat down
and watched the people go by.
Rose drew a picture
of three clowns.

Anna drew a little girl
standing on her hands.
They drew pictures of the rides,
the tables, and some of the people.
"I'm tired of drawing,"
Anna said to Rose.
"Let's take a walk."
"There's Ben," Rose shouted.

He was talking to Mrs. Sanchez.

"Maria must be lost,"

Mrs. Sanchez cried.

"I'm so worried.

I just talked to her mother.

She left home over an hour ago."

"What does she look like?"

asked Ben.

"She's about the size of Rose,"
said Mrs. Sanchez.
"Her mother told me
she was wearing a red tee shirt,
blue jeans, and a green ribbon
on her ponytail."
"Oh," cried Anna.
"I drew her picture.
Here it is."
She showed Mrs. Sanchez
the picture of the girl
standing on her hands.

DRAWINGS of the
FAIR bY ROSE
and ANNA
10¢each

"Good," said Ben.
"She must be here.
We will find her."
"We'll help you look,"
Rose and Anna told Ben.
"Where do we look first?"
Anna asked Rose.

THE TERRIBLE TOWER

"There are so many people,
I can't see," said Anna.
"I can't see either," said Rose.
"We need to be up high
to look for Maria."
"The rides!" cried Anna.
They ran to the Terrible Tower
and told Rose's father
that Maria was missing.

"Get on the Terrible Tower,"
he said.
"Maybe you could see her
from up there."
"You look to the right,"
said Rose.
"I'll look to the left."
The girls looked around
as they went up into the air.
"There she is," shouted Anna,
"by the ice-cream stand."

When the ride came down,
the girls got off
and ran to the stand.
But Maria had gone.
"She moves fast," said Rose.
"I'm hungry," said Anna.

"I know what we need," said Rose.
They each bought
a big ice-cream cone.
"Come on, Rose," said Anna.
"We can look for Maria
while we eat."

The girls looked everywhere,
but they did not find her.
They did find Ben.
"We saw Maria
at the ice-cream stand,"
they told him.

"But we were up high
on the Terrible Tower.
When we got off,
she was gone."
"Keep looking," said Ben.
"We'll find her."

The girls looked some more,
but they did not see Maria again.
"We've only sold two pictures,"
said Rose.
"Let's sell some more,"
Anna said.
"We can look for Maria later."
They went back to their table.

Mike bought a picture
of the three clowns.
Ben bought a picture
of a little dog doing tricks.

Rose's father bought a picture
of the Terrible Tower.
He paid for it
with two tickets for the ride.

"Let's go," shouted Rose.
"Maybe we'll see Maria again,"
said Anna.

They got on the ride
and looked around.
"There's Maria," shouted Anna.
"Where?" asked Rose.
"Up in the air.
Look!" said Anna.
They shouted to Maria,
but she did not hear them.
When Rose and Anna
were up in the air,
they saw Maria get off below.
"There she goes again,"
said Rose.
"She sure gets around fast."
"Let's go and tell Mrs. Sanchez
that we saw Maria,"
said Anna.

Mrs. Sanchez wasn't at her table.

The girls walked down the street,

looking for her.

"Look," said Rose,

"at all those people around our table."

"What are they doing?" asked Anna.
"There's someone drawing
on your sketch pad,"
said Rose.
"It's Maria," they shouted.

"Hi, Maria!"
the girls said together.
"I'm Anna and this is Rose.
And that's my sketch pad."
"I hope you didn't mind,"
said Maria.
"I like to draw too.
You weren't here,
so I've been drawing
and selling some pictures."
She showed the girls the money.
"Great!" said Anna.
"We'll all buy hot dogs for supper."
"But first," said Rose,
"we have to find Mrs. Sanchez.
She'll be happy
you aren't lost anymore."

DRAWINGS of the
FAIR by Rose
and ANNA
10¢ each

"I've been looking for her too,"
said Maria.
"When I couldn't find her,
I left a note on her door."
Just then
Mrs. Sanchez ran over
and hugged Maria.

"I found your note,
so I knew you were OK,"
she said.
"We found her,"
the girls said to Mrs. Sanchez.
Mrs. Sanchez hugged
Rose and Anna too.

Just then Ben came by.
"We found Maria,"
the girls shouted.
"Here she is!"
"You're good artists
and good detectives,"
Ben told the girls.

"I'm glad Maria is found."
The fair was almost over.
"Fairs make me hungry,"
said Anna.
"Me too," said Maria.
"Let's go buy those hot dogs,"
said Rose.

After the girls had eaten,
Rose's father asked,
"How about one last ride?"
"Yay!" shouted Maria.
"Let's get on,"
said Rose and Anna.
It was the longest
and the best ride of all.
When they got off,
Maria's mother was waiting for her.

"Can you come
and play with me next week?"
Maria asked the girls.
"Sure, we'd love to," said Anna.
"If we can find you!" said Rose.
Everyone laughed.

BOOK CHARGING CARD

watts

Accession No. _____ Call No. _____

Author _____

Title _____ Where is Maria _____

Date Loaned	Borrower's Name	Date Returned

SEP
SEP
OCT
OCT
D
JA
JA
F

7584